Thomas the Tank Engine & Friends™

CREATED BY BRITT ALLCROFT
Based on the Railway Series by the Reverend W Awdry
Compilation copyright © 2016 Gullane (Thomas) LLC.
Thomas the Tank Engine & Friends and Thomas & Friends are trademarks of Gullane
(Thomas) Limited. Thomas the Tank Engine & Friends and Design Is Reg. U.S. Pat.
& Tm. Off. © 2016 HIT Entertainment Limited. All rights reserved. Published in the
United States by Random House Children's Books, a division of Penguin Random House
LLC, 1745 Broadway, New York, NY 10019, and in Canada by Penguin Random House
Canada Limited, Toronto. Random House and the colophon are registered trademarks
of Penguin Random House LLC.

This compilation contains the following twelve works previously published in Great
Britain by Egmont UK Limited:
"Busy Engines" © 2012 Gullane (Thomas) LLC
"The Lost Puff" © 2014 Gullane (Thomas) LLC
"Thomas and Scruff" © 2012 Gullane (Thomas) LLC
"Percy's New Friends" © 2012 Gullane (Thomas) LLC
"Don't Bother Victor!" © 2013 Gullane (Thomas) LLC
"On Misty Island" © 2012 Gullane (Thomas) LLC
"James to the Rescue" © 2012 Gullane (Thomas) LLC
"Belle's New Friend" © 2012 Gullane (Thomas) LLC
"Edward the Hero" © 2012 Gullane (Thomas) LLC
"Gordon Runs Dry" © 2014 Gullane (Thomas) LLC
"Noisy Stafford" © 2014 Gullane (Thomas) LLC
"Kevin Meets Cranky" © 2014 Gullane (Thomas) LLC

Visit us on the Web!
randomhousekids.com
www.thomasandfriends.com
Educators and librarians, for a variety of teaching tools,
visit us at RHTeachersLibrarians.com

ISBN 978-0-399-55207-6 (trade) — ISBN 978-0-399-55208-3 (ebook)

MANUFACTURED IN CHINA
20 19 18 17 16 15 14 13 12 11

HiT entertainment

5-Minute Stories

The Sleepytime Collection

Based on the Railway Series
by the Reverend W Awdry

Random House 🏠 New York

CONTENTS

STORY 1

Busy Engines

It was a special day on Sodor. The Railway Inspector was coming to inspect Sir Topham Hatt's Railway!

"Thomas, you should be shunting coal trucks when the Inspector arrives," said Sir Topham Hatt. "He wants to see busy engines! It's very important!"

Thomas went to find some of his engine friends. He wanted to ask them to help shunt trucks.

He puffed to Maron Station. Percy was there, waiting for the mail.

"Hello, Percy," peeped Thomas. "Will you come and shunt coal trucks with me? The Inspector is arriving soon, and he wants to see busy engines!"

Percy was supposed to deliver the mail, but he did want to help Thomas, too. Percy was uncoupled and away he whooshed.

And where did the Inspector go first?
To Maron Station!

When the Inspector arrived to check on things, Percy
wasn't there! The Inspector was *not* very pleased.

In the meantime, Thomas huffed to the Quarry, where Mavis was waiting to pull some slate trucks.

"Will you come and shunt coal trucks?" peeped Thomas. "The Inspector is due to arrive, and he wants to see busy engines!"

Mavis had a lot to do, but she decided to help Thomas, too.

And where do you think the Inspector went next?
The Quarry!

When he arrived at the Quarry, Mavis wasn't there.
Uh-oh!

The Inspector was not pleased at all!

Thomas was chuffing cheerily back to the Docks.

Percy and Mavis had already shunted a long line of coal trucks. They knew that the Inspector would be so pleased!

Then Thomas heard Gordon's whistle go "*Peep!*" as he delivered the Inspector to the Docks.

"We must look busy!" Thomas said urgently.

So Percy shoved. And Mavis shunted. And the coal trucks biffed and bashed together!

And then—oh, no! Coal dust flew down Gordon's funnel. It made him sputter and splutter and cough. The dust flew back out of his funnel and landed everywhere!

Sir Topham Hatt was very cross. "What's going on?" he shouted. "Thomas, what have you been up to? The Inspector is not pleased at all!" Poor Thomas! He felt terrible.

Thomas knew he had to make things right. He heaved and hauled Gordon to the Steamworks for repair.

Soon Gordon's funnel was fixed and his firebox was roaring away again.

Thomas steamed back to the Docks. He was ready to be a very busy engine. He shunted and shoved until all the trucks were in the right places. He was so busy that he didn't notice that Sir Topham Hatt and the Inspector were watching him.

"You've been a very busy engine," the Inspector said to Thomas.

"Next time, Thomas," said Sir Topham Hatt, "remember that you can be a busy engine all by yourself—and a Really Useful one, too."

"Oh, I will, Sir," Thomas replied. "I certainly will!"

And he beamed from buffer to buffer!

STORY 2
The Lost Puff

One day, Sir Topham Hatt told the engines that there was some damaged track at Knapford Bend.

All the engines on the Railway listened carefully, except Paxton and Thomas, who were laughing at the antics of a duck that was waddling toward the Sheds.

"May I remind you two in particular not to be silly," Sir Topham Hatt said sternly. "You must pay attention. I don't want any accidents!"

A little while later, Paxton arrived at the broken track.
As he rolled over it, it rattled his radiator, making him
laugh.

"That was fun!" he said, grinning.

When Thomas arrived at the bend, Paxton got him to
try it, too.

"Woo-hooooo!" Thomas said with a giggle as he
bounced along.

"Get up some speed and go over it really fast," Paxton suggested.

So Thomas raced backward around the corner and—oops!—bashed right into Toby, who was filling up at the water tower.

Water splashed all over—and all over Thomas. It put out his firebox.

"Oh, no!" Paxton cried. "Sir Topham Hatt told me not to be silly, but I was, and now there's been an accident."

Paxton rolled away quickly and quietly to deliver his trucks to the Shunting Yards.

When Toby arrived at the Shunting Yards, Paxton heard him tell Stafford that Thomas had lost his puff. That sounded serious!

Paxton decided that he would go and look for Thomas' lost puff. He would find it! He raced along, looking all around, but he didn't really know what to look for.

Then he saw a puff of steam and raced after it. But it turned out to be just Gordon, pulling the Express.

Next, Paxton spotted a fluffy white cloud in the sky.

"*That* must be Thomas' missing puff!" he said as he hurried toward it.

Paxton followed the cloud all the way to Ulfstead Castle, where he met Stephen.

"Hello, Paxton," Stephen said. "What are you doing here?"

"Thomas has lost his puff, and I thought that might be it," Paxton told him, looking up at the cloud.

"Up there? That's just a cloud," Stephen replied.

Paxton felt rather silly. He sped away as fast as his wheels could carry him.

Paxton realized he didn't know anything about a steam engine's puff because he was a diesel engine. But he knew someone who *did* know about steam engines—Victor, whose job it was to repair them!

Paxton hurried to the Steamworks to find Victor. He
asked Victor if he had a spare puff for Thomas. This made
Toby, who was at the Steamworks for repairs, laugh.

"Puff just means steam," Toby explained to Paxton.
"When Thomas bumped into me, his firebox got wet.
Steamies can't make puffs when their fire goes out."

Once again, Paxton felt silly. But he cheered up again when he realized that Thomas would be fine, just as soon as his firebox dried out.

As Paxton sped back to the water tower, he heard a cheerful *"Peep!"* And there was Thomas, puffing around the corner.

"You're okay!" Paxton said happily.

"Yes, I found my lost puff!" Thomas joked.

"At least I learned something today," Paxton said, smiling.

"That *puff* just means '*steam*'?" asked Thomas.

"Yes," Paxton said, still smiling, "But also that when Sir Topham Hatt tells me not to be silly, I shouldn't be silly!"

And Thomas wholeheartedly agreed.

╫╫╫╫╫╫╫ **STORY 3** ╫╫╫╫╫╫╫

Thomas and Scruff

Thomas' friend Whiff worked at the waste dump on the Island of Sodor, biffing and bashing trucks full of trash. Keeping Sodor clean and tidy was a *lot* of work! It was a very important job.

One day, Thomas went to tell Whiff some good news.
"I'm fetching a helper for you," he peeped.
Whiff was very excited to hear this.

Thomas steamed to the Docks to meet Scruff the Scruncher.

"Hello, Thomas," Scruff chuffed. "I can't wait to scrunch some trash!"

Thomas liked Scruff. He thought he was very nice. But he also thought Scruff looked very dirty.

An idea flew into Thomas'
funnel. He asked Scruff to wait
right there for a special surprise.
Then Thomas chuffed away to
gather some brushes and buckets
and soap and sponges.

Back at the Docks, Thomas showed Scruff his surprise.
"With a splish and a splash, you'll be clean in a dash!"
he peeped.

But Scruff was scared. He had never seen soap or
brushes before. He did not like this surprise at all!

With a clickety-clack, Scruff whooshed away and hid in a siding.

Thomas realized that Scruff was scared of being washed. "Please come out, Scruff!" he called.

But Scruff refused to come out of hiding.

Thomas asked Gordon to see if he could get Scruff out of the siding.

"Scruff, would you like to see my Express carriages?" Gordon asked. "They're green and very grand!"

But Scruff didn't want to see the carriages. He stayed right where he was.

Next, Thomas asked Henry to try.

"Scruff, would you like to help fetch my special coal?" Henry huffed. "It makes me fast and fearless!"

But Scruff didn't want to fetch any coal. He was not going to come out of that siding.

After that, Thomas asked Percy to give it a try.

"Scruff, would you like to pull my mail trucks?"
Percy peeped. "They're packed with parcels!"

But Scruff didn't want to
pull the mail trucks. He just
stayed put.

Finally, Thomas remembered the one thing that Scruff *did* want to do.

"Scruff, would you like to go and scrunch some trash at the waste dump?" Thomas asked. "You don't have to be clean for that."

When he heard what Thomas said, Scruff wheeshed quickly out of the siding. He was ready to go!

Thomas and Scruff steamed off to the waste dump, where Whiff was waiting for them. Scruff looked around at the dirty dump.

"I'm going to like it here," he whistled. "There isn't any soap! And no water and brushes, either!"

He laughed happily, and Thomas and Whiff laughed with him.

THOMAS & FRIENDS™

╫╫╫╫╫╫╫ **STORY 4** ╫╫╫╫╫╫╫

Percy's New Friends

It was a very busy day on Sodor. All the engines were huffing and puffing as they worked—all except for Percy.

Percy wasn't busy. He wanted to play. But all the other engines were too busy to play with Percy.

Percy puffed sadly to Brendam Docks.

At the Docks, a noisy bird was squawking loudly as it sat on Cranky's arm.

"Hello, Percy," said Cranky. "This is my friend Seagull."

An idea flew into Percy's funnel.

"I could make friends with animals, too!" Percy thought.

And he clattered away to make some new friends.

The noise scared Seagull. Away he flew.

"Not so loud, Percy!" Cranky warned. But Percy didn't hear.

Percy puffed into the woods. There he saw
a rabbit. With a wheesh and a whoosh and a
hoot and a toot, Percy rushed to make friends.

But the rabbit was frightened. It turned tail
and raced away into the bushes!

Farther down the track, Percy saw some squirrels. With a wheesh and a whoosh and a hoot and a toot, Percy rushed to make friends.

But the startled squirrels scurried away up a tree with their bushy tails waving.

Percy chuffed on through the woods until he saw a bird.

Again, he rushed to make friends. But the bird squawked loudly and flew off.

Percy was puzzled. Why didn't any of the animals want to be his friend?

Suddenly, Percy heard the roar of an engine and the loud wheeeep of a warning whistle.

"Bust my buffers!" cried Percy. He was frightened through and through.

It was Gordon, pulling the Express!

Percy shook from funnel to footplate as Gordon thundered past.

Thomas happened to be nearby and saw what had happened. "Are you okay?" he asked Percy.

"I was scared," Percy said. "Gordon is big, and I'm only a little engine."

Then, suddenly, an idea bubbled up in Percy's boiler.

Percy set off, back through the woods. This time, he puffed slowly and carefully. Soon he saw the little bird.

"Hello," Percy said quietly.

"Cheep, cheep," the bird replied, and he flew onto Percy's buffer.

Percy puffed on, carefully and calmly. Next he saw the squirrels.

"Hello, Mr. and Mrs. Squirrel," he said softly. "I didn't mean to scare you before."

The squirrels leaped onto Percy's buffer, too.

Finally, Percy saw the rabbit again.

"I'm sorry for being too loud before," he said to the bunny.

The rabbit twitched its nose and hopped up next to the squirrels.

Percy puffed proudly on with all of his new friends. He was the happiest engine on Sodor!

======== **STORY 5** ========
Don't Bother Victor

One day, up in the hills on the Island of Sodor, Thomas saw Peter Sam and Mr. Percival.

"I'm off to meet Sir Topham Hatt today," said Mr. Percival. "So I'm putting you in charge for the day, Peter Sam."

Peter Sam gasped. "Me, Sir?" he said. "I'll take good care of things. You can be sure of that!"

Mr. Percival told Peter Sam that Victor would be coming by later that day. Victor was in charge of repairs at the Steamworks, and he was a very important engine.

"Don't go bothering him before then with little things," said Mr. Percival.

"Good luck, Peter Sam!" Thomas said as he started to chug away. "Being in charge is fun. *You* get to make all the decisions!"

Thomas took Mr. Percival to meet Sir Topham Hatt. Peter Sam was now in charge.

Just then, Rheneas chuffed along. "Sir Handel is creaking and groaning at Daisy Halt," he said to Peter Sam. "You must fetch Victor to mend him!"

Peter Sam looked serious. "No, Rheneas," he said firmly. "We must not bother Victor with little things. I will fix Sir Handel myself!"

When Peter Sam arrived at Daisy Halt, Sir Handel was indeed creaking and groaning.

"Please fetch Victor!" he said to Peter Sam.

"I'm sure I can fix you," said Peter Sam. "I think you just need more oil."

So Sir Handel's Driver added more oil. But Sir Handel creaked more than ever!

Just then, Rheneas came along.

"Now Skarloey's funnel is broken!" he reported.
"Peter Sam, you *must* fetch Victor!"

"We must *not* bother Victor!" Peter Sam replied.
"I will chuff over to Skarloey and fix him myself."

And off he puffed, leaving Sir Handel behind.

Skarloey was wheeshing with worry. "My funnel is blocked!" he said. "Please fetch Victor!"

"Don't worry, Skarloey. I'm sure I can fix you," said Peter Sam. He thought hard. "We need to put some water down your funnel."

So Skarloey's Driver put water down his funnel. But that only made things worse!

"All that water has put my firebox out!" Skarloey cried.

Peter Sam was upset. He realized that he hadn't done a very good job of being in charge. He puffed along sadly until he came to a stop himself.

"Oh, no!" he groaned. "Now I've run out of coal!"

Luckily, Rheneas came by and found Peter Sam.

"I've run out of coal!" Peter Sam told him.
"Please fetch Victor!"

Rheneas chuckled. "But *you* said we shouldn't
bother Victor."

Then Peter Sam remembered what Thomas had
told him.

"When *you* are in charge, *you* get to make all the
decisions!" Peter Sam said out loud. "Rheneas—I've
decided we *can* bother Victor!"

Victor managed to fix all the broken engines. "Why didn't you come and get me earlier?" he asked.

"Mr. Percival said not to bother you," Peter Sam told him.

"I don't mind," said Victor. "It's my job to fix Really Useful Engines."

Later that day, Thomas brought Mr. Percival back to the hills. "How was your day in charge, Peter Sam?" he asked.

"No bother at all!" Peter Sam replied. "Don't you agree, Victor?"

"I do, indeed," Victor answered. "It was no bother at all!"

STORY 6
On Misty Island

One day, Thomas and Edward were given a very special job. They were to bring Jobi wood from Misty Island back to Sodor.

"You'll need our help," Bash and Dash told Thomas. "The log loaders can be very naughty. We're used to working with them."

"That's right," Ferdinand added.

But Thomas had been to Misty Island before, and he thought he knew all about it. He didn't need any help!

When Thomas and Edward got to Misty Island, Thomas showed Edward around, and then led the way to the Shake-Shake Bridge. The Logging Station was just on the other side.

As the two engines crossed the bridge, it wibbled and wobbled under their wheels. Edward was scared! He stopped halfway across and refused to budge another inch.

"Don't worry, Edward," Thomas said. "I'll fetch the logs. Then we can take them right back to Sodor."

At the Logging Station, Ol' Wheezy, the naughty log loader, picked up some Jobi logs. But instead of putting them onto Thomas' truck, he whirled around and hurled them up into the air. The logs flew everywhere!

"Blistering boilers!" cried Edward as the logs flew toward him. They bounced off his cab and made the Shake-Shake Bridge shake even more! Edward was more scared than ever!

As Ol' Wheezy was throwing
around another batch of logs, Bash,
Dash, and Ferdinand puffed in.

"It looks like you need our help
now," Bash and Dash said.

"That's right!" said Ferdinand.

But Thomas still thought he didn't
need any help, so the other engines
rolled away again.

Thomas chuffed over to Hee Haw, the other log
loader. But Hee Haw was feeling too sick to work.

Just then, James arrived with Sir Topham Hatt.
Hee Haw wheeshed and wheezed and coughed black
smoke all over them!

"Thomas!" Sir Topham Hatt boomed crossly. "Logs are flying everywhere, Edward won't move, and you are late with your delivery!"

Thomas felt terrible. "I'm sorry, Sir," he peeped. "I thought I didn't need help here, but I was wrong. Now I'll make things right!"

Thomas went to find Bash, Dash, and Ferdinand.

"I can't do this alone after all," he puffed. "I need your help."

"Do as we say and we'll show you the way!" chuffed Bash and Dash together.

"That's right!" said Ferdinand, as he usually did.

Together the engines steamed back to the Logging Station.

First, the three locomotives pushed Edward across the Shake-Shake Bridge.

Next, they oiled Hee Haw's joints to make him feel better.

Then they gathered up the logs that Ol' Wheezy had thrown into the air.

Soon all the trucks were piled high with Jobi wood.

When the five engines returned to Sodor with the wood, Sir Topham Hatt was very pleased. "You are Really Useful Engines," he told them.

"We make a great team!" whistled Bash and Dash.

"That's right!" Ferdinand, Thomas, and Edward peeped all together.

STORY 7

James to the Rescue

One lovely morning, James pulled into Sodor's Search and Rescue Center. He was smiling widely and looking very pleased.

"Sir Topham Hatt has asked me to be the Rescue Engine today!" he puffed proudly to Rocky.

Just then, Toby trundled up the track. "Hello,
James," he tooted. "Sir Topham Hatt has sent me
to help you."

But James most certainly didn't want any help.

At that very moment, Rocky received an urgent message from Gordon's Driver. Gordon was in trouble!

James immediately puffed away down the track to rescue his friend.

"Wait for me!" Toby tooted. "Remember—Gordon's a big engine. You're going to need some help!"

But James most certainly didn't want any help.
Gordon's front wheels had come off the track.

"I'll shunt you back onto the track in no time!"
James peeped.

Toby was worried. "Gordon's a heavy engine,"
he said. "We should fetch Rocky for this job."

But James most certainly didn't want any help.

"I'm the Rescue Engine," he puffed proudly. "I can do this myself."

James buffered up behind the big blue engine. He shoved, and he shunted. And then there was trouble!

The track creaked. It cracked. And then . . .
it crumbled!

Gordon groaned as the track gave way.

"I think now it really is time to get Rocky," Toby told James.

But James *still* didn't want any help!

"*I'm* the Rescue Engine, and I have a plan!" he peeped. "I'll biff Gordon back onto the track!"

So James backed up behind Gordon. Then he pumped his pistons. And then he biffed Gordon's buffer with a huge bash!

But—oh, no!—James and Gordon toppled off the track together into a muddy field!

"I guess I'm not a very good Rescue Engine, after all," James said sadly. "And now I really do need help."

"Happy to help, James!" Toby peeped proudly. He rushed back to the Rescue Center to fetch Rocky.

Rocky came and lifted Gordon and James
out of the mud and back onto the track.

"Toby, will you please shunt me to the Rescue Center?" James asked.

"Happy to help, James!" Toby peeped proudly again.

Back at the Rescue Center, Sir Topham Hatt was waiting for James and Toby.

"Thank you for sending Toby to help me, Sir," James said. "You'll be glad to know that he's the best Rescue Tram on Sodor."

And Toby was glad to hear it. He beamed from buffer to buffer!

Edward the Hero

One day, Edward pulled into Knapford Station, where he saw Thomas. Thomas was very excited.

"Sir Topham Hatt has an important job for you,"
Thomas peeped. "He wants you to work with Harold as
the Rescue Engine. You will be Edward the Hero!"

Edward thought that he would like to be a
hero. But he was worried. He wasn't sure that
he'd be very good at it. In fact, he didn't have
any idea *how* to be a hero.

Just then, Gordon raced through the station, pushing Rocky. Gordon was strong and fast and stern.

"Gordon is a hero," Edward thought. "I must be more like him." And he puffed out of the station.

But as Edward went along trying to be strong and fast and stern, he saw Charlie looking sad. Charlie had forgotten all the jokes he wanted to tell the children.

So Edward told Charlie some more jokes and made him jiggle and giggle.

"You're *funny*!" chuffed Charlie.

That made Edward happy. But then he remembered something. . . .

"Oh, dear," he said with a sigh. "I wasn't strong or fast or stern. I was just funny. I must try harder to be a hero."

Farther along the line, Dowager Hatt stood on the platform, looking worried.

She had sent her suitcase to Maron Station by mistake. Edward raced to fetch it and brought it safely back to her.

"You are very kind," Dowager Hatt said to Edward.

"Just kind?" Edward said, sighing again. "I must try harder to be a hero."

Then Edward saw Farmer
McColl's little dog. He was
lost, and he was scared of
the engine.

Very gently, Edward edged
closer. The dog jumped
aboard, and Edward took
him back to Farmer McColl.

"You were very gentle, Edward," Farmer McColl said happily. "Thank you."

"Oh, dear," Edward puffed. "I was just gentle. I wasn't strong or fast or stern. I must try harder to be a hero."

When Edward finally arrived at the Rescue Center, Harold wasn't there.

"He must have left without me," Edward said sadly. "I'm not strong or fast or stern."

Edward slowly puffed back to Knapford Station to tell Sir Topham Hatt that he just wasn't a hero.

On the way there, he passed Farmer McColl, who called out, "There he is! Edward the Hero!"

A little later, he passed Charlie, who called out the same thing: "There he is! Edward the Hero!"

Edward didn't understand.

When he arrived at Knapford Station, Dowager Hatt was there. She called out, "There he is! Edward the Hero!"

"But I'm not a hero," Edward said. "I wasn't strong or fast or stern."

"No, you weren't," replied Sir Topham Hatt. "You were kind and funny and gentle. You are a hero, Edward, just being yourself!"

And Edward beamed from buffer to buffer.

STORY 9
Belle's New Friend

Everyone on Sodor liked the new engine, Belle.
She was a big blue engine with a big bell. Belle could
fight fires with a whoosh of water.

One day, Thomas puffed into Knapford Station and saw Belle watching Toby as he trundled away.

"Who's that, Thomas?" Belle asked. "He has a bell, too. I'm sure we could be good friends."

Thomas told Belle all about Toby. He also told her where to find Toby's hut.

Belle wheeshed straight to Toby's hut. Belle was big and noisy. She made Toby feel very small. Toby told Belle that he liked to be quiet and to listen to the birds singing.

"I know how we can have much more fun than that," said Belle. "Follow me!"

Belle took Toby to the bottom of a hill.

"Let's race to the top and then whoosh down!" she cried. Off she puffed at full speed.

"That was fun!" Belle said, laughing as she came to a stop.

But Toby didn't answer—because Toby wasn't there!

"I'm not good at racing," Toby said when Belle found him.

"Don't worry," Belle replied. She really wanted Toby to have fun.

And she really wanted him to be her friend.

"I know what we'll do," she said. She raced off to a field full of pigs as Toby followed.

"I like pigs," said Toby. "They make me happy."

That made Belle happy, too! Then she had an idea.

"Pigs like mud, don't they?" she asked. She whooshed water from her spouts into the field.

But Toby didn't answer, because Toby wasn't there.

"I don't like whooshing water,"
Toby explained when Belle found him.
"Don't worry," she replied. "Follow me!"
Belle chuffed off to Maithwaite Station
and rang her big loud bell—Ding-ding!
Ding-ding!—for all the waiting passengers
to hear.

"We're the bells of Sodor," Belle said, laughing merrily. "Ring your bell for the passengers, too, Toby!"

But Toby didn't answer, because Toby wasn't there. Belle was worried. She wanted to find Toby. She wheeshed away to look for him.

Belle found Toby hiding in his shed.

"You didn't have any fun," she said to him sadly. "And now you won't want to be my friend."

They both sat quietly. Belle heard the birds singing.

"That's a beautiful sound," she said.

Toby smiled.

Then Toby had an idea. He took Belle back to the pigs.

Quietly, they watched the pigs snorting and snuffling.

Belle didn't make Toby feel small anymore.

Then Belle and Toby went back to Maithwaite Station. Toby jingled and jangled his bell for the passengers.

Belle rang her big bell as quietly as she could.

"Belle is my friend," Toby told everyone. "We're the bells of Sodor!"

And Belle smiled from buffer to buffer.

THOMAS & FRIENDS™

STORY 10
Gordon Runs Dry

One morning on the Island of Sodor, Gordon's coaches were late.

"I shouldn't be kept waiting," he moaned. "The Express is the most important train on the Island."

Thomas thought local trains were important, too, but Gordon didn't agree.

At last, Gordon was coupled to the Express and he rushed off to the Main Line.

Farther along the track, Paxton was pulling stone trucks. He didn't know that Gordon was hurrying toward him.

Suddenly, Paxton's signal turned red.

As Paxton braked, a stone flew out of his truck. It hit Gordon's boiler!

"I'm so sorry," Paxton said with a gasp. "Are you okay?"

"I'm fine," Gordon replied. "You can't damage a strong engine like me so easily."

"You should get checked for damage, just in case," Paxton warned him.

"Nonsense!" Gordon replied. "The Express must not be late!"

But Gordon didn't get far before his boiler began to run dry.

"That's funny," he said to himself. "I thought I had plenty of water."

So when he saw a water tower, Gordon asked his Driver to stop and fill up his tank.

But Gordon didn't get much farther than that before his boiler felt hot and dry again.

"I can't stop twice," he fretted. "I'll be late. I *must* keep going. This is the Express!"

Thirsty Gordon tried to ignore the river he passed, but with his boiler running dry again, he had to stop at the next water tower.

Gordon's passengers weren't happy. The Express was meant to be a fast train, not a slow one!

"I'll be fast now!" Gordon promised as he hurried to Wellsworth Station.

But as soon as he was back on the Main Line, his boiler felt dry again.

Poor Gordon left a wet trail behind him as he went slower and slower and finally came to a stop.

Thomas followed the wet trail along the track—and found Gordon.

"I've run out of steam," Gordon said sadly.

"You must have a leak," Thomas said.

Gordon wondered how that could have happened.

It was when Paxton arrived that Gordon remembered the accident.

"I *should* have been checked after that stone hit me," Gordon said to him.

Then Thomas saw the hole in Gordon's boiler.

"Don't worry, Gordon," he said. "I'll take your passengers, and Paxton can push you to the Steamworks to be fixed." He smiled at Gordon.

Later that day, Gordon pulled into Knapford
Station blowing steam from his mended boiler.

The other engines teased him, but Gordon had
learned his lesson. In the future, he would always
make sure to take care of his boiler.

STORY 11
Noisy Stafford

Lots of engines on the Island of Sodor are noisy steam engines like Thomas and Percy.

But Stafford is quiet because he is a battery-powered electric engine.

One day, Stafford saw some
children waving from a bridge as
Thomas and Percy tooted and peeped
below them.

But when Stafford gently hummed past, the children
wondered why he was so quiet.

A little later, Stafford met Thomas and Percy on the Main Line.

"I know I'm an electric engine," Stafford said to them, "but I want to chuff and puff loudly like a steam engine."

"We'll teach you!" Thomas said with a smile.

"Chuff, chuff, chuff! Puff, puff, puff!" Stafford said, copying Thomas and Percy.

"Well done, Stafford," said Percy. "You sound just like a Steamie!"

Stafford beamed happily as he raced away.

At Brendam Docks, Stafford heard Henry wheeshing loudly.

"Ohhh!" said Stafford. "That's another Steamie sound I'm going to make!"

And he also copied Gordon, who honked his horn and blew his whistle—"Woooo-wooo!"

The next time Stafford passed the children on the bridge, he made all the Steamie noises: *Puff, puff, puff! Chuff, chuff, chuff! Wheesh! Woooo-wooo!*

The children cheered with delight.

When Stafford went to the Yard to charge his battery, Sir Topham Hatt was there. He had an urgent job for Stafford.

"You're needed at Farmer McColl's farm," Sir Topham Hatt said. "You're just the engine for the job."

But when Stafford arrived at the farm, making his Steamie sounds, he scared the farmer's sheep.

"I asked for you because you're a quiet engine," Farmer McColl said to Stafford. "But your Steamie noises have made my sheep run away!"

Stafford heard the sheep *ba*aing farther along the track. Quietly, he took Farmer McColl to find them.

Stafford hummed softly as the farmer loaded the sheep into his truck. And he watched happily as they trotted out of his truck into their new field.

"The sheep really like you because you're nice and quiet, Stafford," said Farmer McColl.

Stafford realized that sometimes it was good to be a quiet engine.

Later, when Stafford hummed into the Yard, Thomas and Percy asked him what had happened to his Steamie sounds.

"I'm not making them anymore," Stafford replied. "I'm not Steamie Stafford; I'm Quiet Stafford, the Electric Engine!"

And off he went, hardly making a sound.

Kevin Meets Cranky

Cranky was having a busy day at the Docks. He worked as hard as he could, but more and more cargo kept arriving.

"Lifting and loading—does it ever stop?" he moaned as boxes piled up around him.

Sir Topham Hatt asked Kevin to help Cranky.

Kevin was very excited. "I've always wanted to meet Cranky!" he said with a big smile.

He couldn't wait to show everyone what a Really Useful Crane he was!

"Hello, Cranky," Kevin said when he arrived at the Docks. "I'm here to lend you a helping hook. What do you want me to do?"

"I don't need any help," Cranky replied.

"But surely there's something I can do," Kevin replied.

"Just stay out of my way, then!" Cranky said. "I don't need any help, thank you very much!"

Kevin moved to a quiet corner of the Docks and waited to be called.

"Don't fret, matey. He's Cranky by name and cranky by nature," Salty said kindly. "You'll get used to him."

Then, as Cranky unloaded some pipes from a ship, a few pipes came loose.

"Look out!" he yelled as they crashed down onto the Docks.

"I'll get them," Kevin called. He rushed to help.

Kevin stacked up all the pipes as neatly as he could.

"There you go, Cranky. All done," he said.

But Cranky wasn't happy. "That was *your* fault!" he said. "You're watching me all the time. It makes me nervous. Go away and stop interfering!"

Later, Cranky was carrying a crate of chickens when it cracked open. All the chickens escaped!

"Don't worry—it's all under control," Kevin said as he rounded up the chickens.

"I told you to stay out of my way!" Cranky said, sounding even more annoyed than before. "All your whizzing around is making me dizzy!"

Then Kevin heard a loud crash. Cranky's hook
had knocked over some barrels, and one of them was
rolling toward the water's edge.

"I've got it!" Kevin said as he hurried to reach the
barrel. But he couldn't stop himself, and *he* fell into
the sea instead!

"Help! Help!" Kevin called.

"Crane overboard!" Salty shouted.

Cranky quickly lowered his hook and carefully lifted Kevin out of the sea.

"Well done, matey!" Salty said, smiling.

When Sir Topham Hatt heard what had happened, he was not happy at all!

"I thought I could trust you with this special job, Kevin," he said.

"It wasn't his fault, Sir," Cranky told him. "It was mine. Kevin was only trying to help. He's been a Really Useful Crane."

"Well, it's good to see you getting along so well," Sir Topham Hatt replied. "Carry on!"

"What would you like me to do now?" Kevin asked Cranky.

"Let's get the Docks looking shipshape," Cranky answered.

"Okay, boss!" Kevin said with a big smile. "You and me, Cranky. What a great team!"